ONCE UPON A TIMELESS TALE

Goldilocks and the Three Bears

STORY BY **ROBERT SOUTHEY**
RETOLD BY **MARGRETE LAMOND**,
WITH **RUSSELL THOMSON**

PICTURES BY
ANNA WALKER

LITTLE HARE
www.littleharebooks.com

There was once a girl with hair that shone like gold, and so she was called Goldilocks, because that was the best name for her. She lived in a cottage surrounded by fields of flowers, and beyond the fields was the forest, all around.

Sometimes she would go into the fields to gather flowers, and sometimes she wandered so far she could no longer see her home, and one time Goldilocks wandered so far she ended up in the forest where she had never been before.

So she just kept wandering further into the forest to see what she might see and, after a bit, what did she see but a house in a clearing. It had an upstairs and a downstairs, windows here and there, a front door, and a chimney with smoke coming out—but it didn't seem like a normal house at all.

'I wonder who lives in such an odd house,' Goldilocks said to herself.

So she knocked on the front door to see. When there was no answer she knocked again.

All this knocking made the door swing open, and that was because it hadn't been properly closed by whoever it was that lived there. And because the door was already open, Goldilocks thought she would help it swing open some more.

'Is anybody home?' she asked.

But all she got in reply was a waft of freshly boiled porridge.

'That's strange,' said Goldilocks to herself. 'If there is someone home they should say hello. And if they have gone out they should have shut the door.'

And so, because of this—or because she was fond of porridge—she went inside.

The first thing Goldilocks saw was three bowls steaming away on the kitchen table.

One was a great big bowl, one was a middle-sized not-so-big bowl, and one was a teeny tiny bowl.

'That's a bit strange,' she said to herself. 'If there was someone home, they would be having their breakfast. And if there is no one home, they won't mind if I have it for them.'

Goldilocks picked up a spoon and tried the porridge in the biggest bowl.

'Oh! Too hot!' she said.

So she took a spoonful of porridge from the middle-sized bowl.

'Ugh! Too cold!' she said.

Then she tried a spoonful from the littlest bowl.

'Mmm, just right,' she said, and she ate it all up.

Still there was no one home, but Goldilocks saw three chairs waiting along the wall.

One was a big grand chair, one was a middling-medium not-so-grand chair, and one was a teeny tiny chair.

'I will sit and wait for them to come back,' Goldilocks said to herself.

First she climbed into the big, grand chair.

'Oh, too high!' she said.

So she tried the middling-medium not-so-grand chair.

'Oof, too wide,' she said.

So she tried the teeny tiny chair, and it was just right.

But no sooner did she make herself comfortable than there was a creak and a crackle and a snap, and the chair broke all to pieces.

'Oh-my-goodness-deary-me,' Goldilocks said to herself. 'Now I really must stay and say sorry.'

With nothing more to look at downstairs, she climbed upstairs and found three beds in a row.

One was a great huge big bed. One was a middling-medium not-so-great-huge bed. And one was a teeny tiny bed.

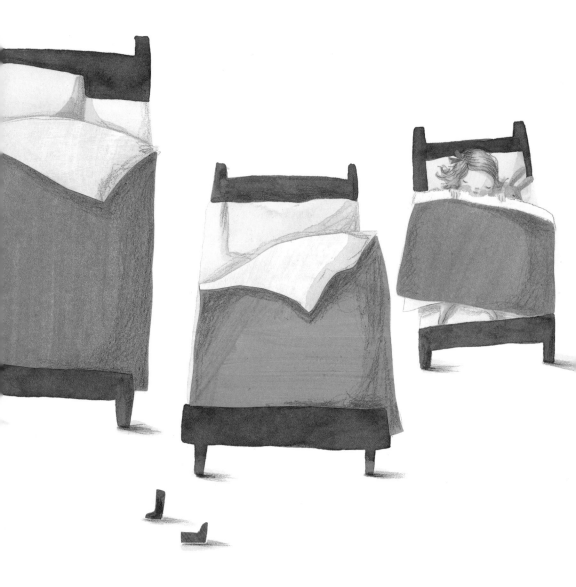

First Goldilocks tried the great huge big bed, but it was too hard.

Next she tried the middling-medium not-so-great-huge bed, but it was too soft.

Then she tried the teeny tiny bed and it was not too hard and not too soft and was altogether so comfortable that she soon fell fast asleep.

While she was sleeping, who should come home but Papa Bear, Mama Bear and Teeny Tiny Baby Bear—because that's whose house it was. They had been for a walk in the forest.

Their porridge was cool at last and now they were hungry and ready for breakfast.

'Look at this!' said Papa Bear. 'Someone's been tasting my porridge!'

'And someone's been tasting my porridge,' said Mama Bear.

'And someone's been tasting my porridge,' wailed Teeny Tiny Baby Bear, 'and they've eaten it all up!'

Then Papa Bear saw something else. 'Someone's been sitting in my chair,' he said.

'And someone's been sitting in my chair,' said Mama Bear.

'And someone's been sitting in my chair,' wailed Teeny Tiny Baby Bear, 'and broken it all to pieces!'

With nothing more to see downstairs, Papa Bear and Mama Bear and Teeny Tiny Baby Bear climbed upstairs, one after the other, to see what they might see.

'Someone's been sleeping in my bed,' said Papa Bear.

'And someone's been sleeping in my bed,' said Mama Bear.

'And someone's been sleeping in my bed,' wailed Teeny Tiny Baby Bear, 'and she's still there!'

Goldilocks woke up with a fright. When she saw the three bears bending over her she screamed and jumped out of the teeny tiny bed. Then she ran down the stairs, out the front door, through the forest and all the way home.

And she never, ever, ever again went to the home of the three bears.

Which was a shame, because they were quite nice, really.

Little Hare Books
an imprint of
Hardie Grant Egmont
Ground Floor, Building 1, 658 Church Street
Richmond, Victoria 3121, Australia

www.littleharebooks.com

First published 2014

Cataloguing-in-Publication details are available from the
National Library of Australia

978 1 921894 92 3 (hbk.)

Designed by Vida & Luke Kelly
Produced by Pica Digital, Singapore
Printed in China by Wai Man Book Binding Ltd.

5 4 3 2 1